In this simplified environment

made mainly of two types

the first of the two types, according to interpretations of rewritten histories, were Jammers.

And then, according to these histories, there was a group called Slammers upon comparison.

They are not the same but they are barely different upon immediate inspection.

immediate inspection

And there are other
inconsequential types
in this environment
that are not to be elaborated upon
until necessary.

The commonly accepted theory within the historical traditions of this environment is that Jammers came before Slammers. But there is no evidence beyond the historical texts to support these claims.

This belief, the "Jammer First" belief, which was written, interpreted and rewritten by ancient Jammers, is the main distinguishing factor between Jammers and Slammers. The more accessible indicator of difference between the two types is the fact that Jammers are of the jamming sort and Slammers choose to be of the slammingness totally.

Rarely does a Jammer or a Slammer deviate from its position as such but, irregularly and usually unintentionally, crossover is achieved.

In the event of a Jammer or a Slammer partaking in the adverse ways of its counterpart, a committee of the Chosen Selected convenes to parpitulate the outcome of the offender's behavioral actions.

Punishments range from the slight

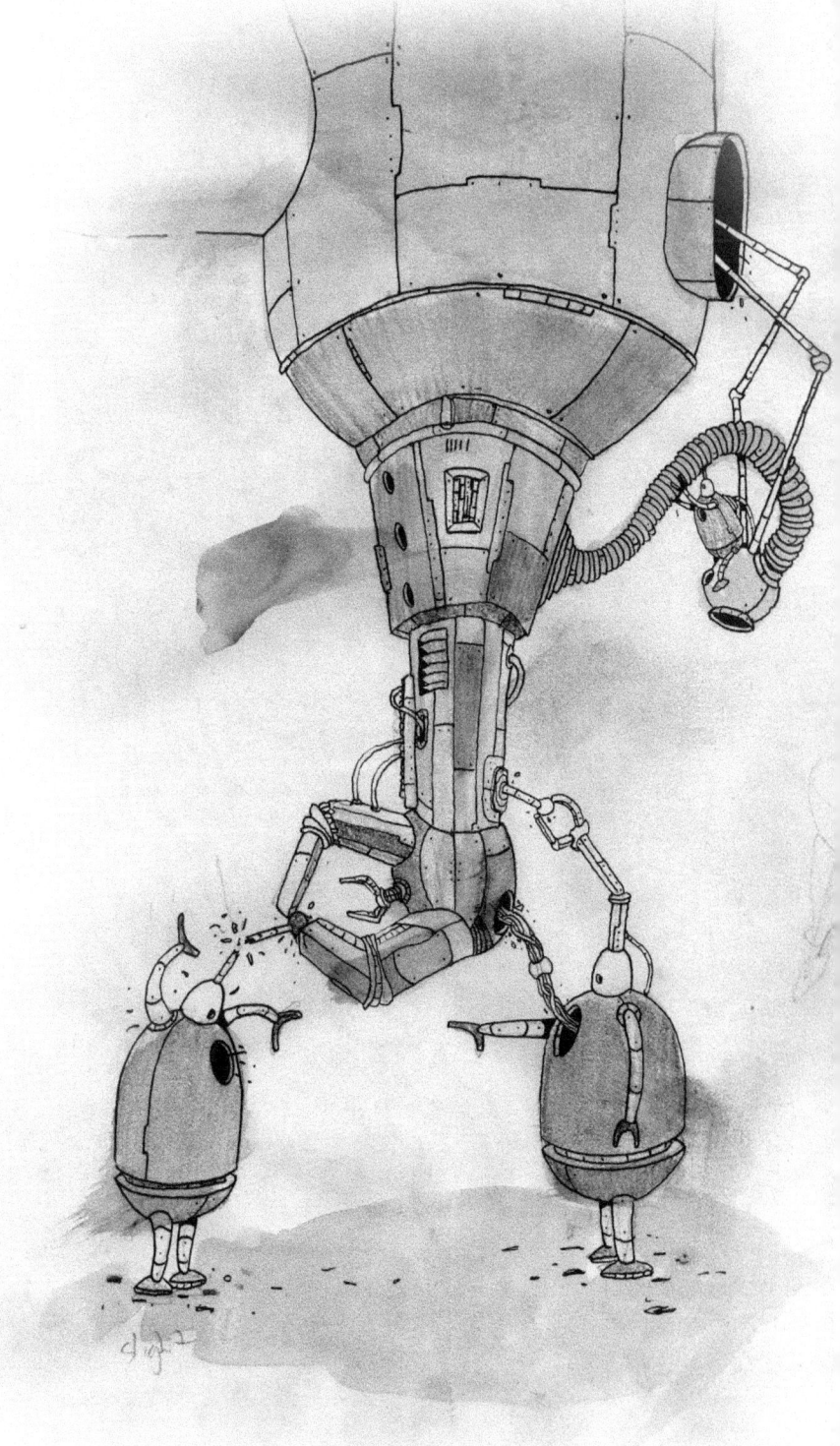

to onwards of excrutionary measures.

Put simply, and again to clarify, Jammers jam and Slammers slam.

again to clarify.

But contrary to the simplicity of the obvious external biopic nature of this environment, there lies within each system a spectral wealth of complexities that are nearly indescribable in their subtleties without attentive witness.

The motivational range of—and almost infinite intricacies within—the nuanced evolution of each of these set Jammer and Slammer systems has been highly specified and refined over lifetimes of generations of interpretational molding to the present state of their individual magnitudes.

The particular set of standard jammings to which Jammers procure themselves involves a system of layers too deep to fully illustrate within this simplified environment.

Attempts have been made.

And it's a secret so the Slammers won't find out, and visa versa.

seco risa vos.

There are however many known motivations and combinational permutations of motivations behind jamming that are accessible knowledge for parties not of the Jammward Order. One of the rarest yet most appreciated jamming motivations is that of Jammers jamming for the sheer delight of jamming.

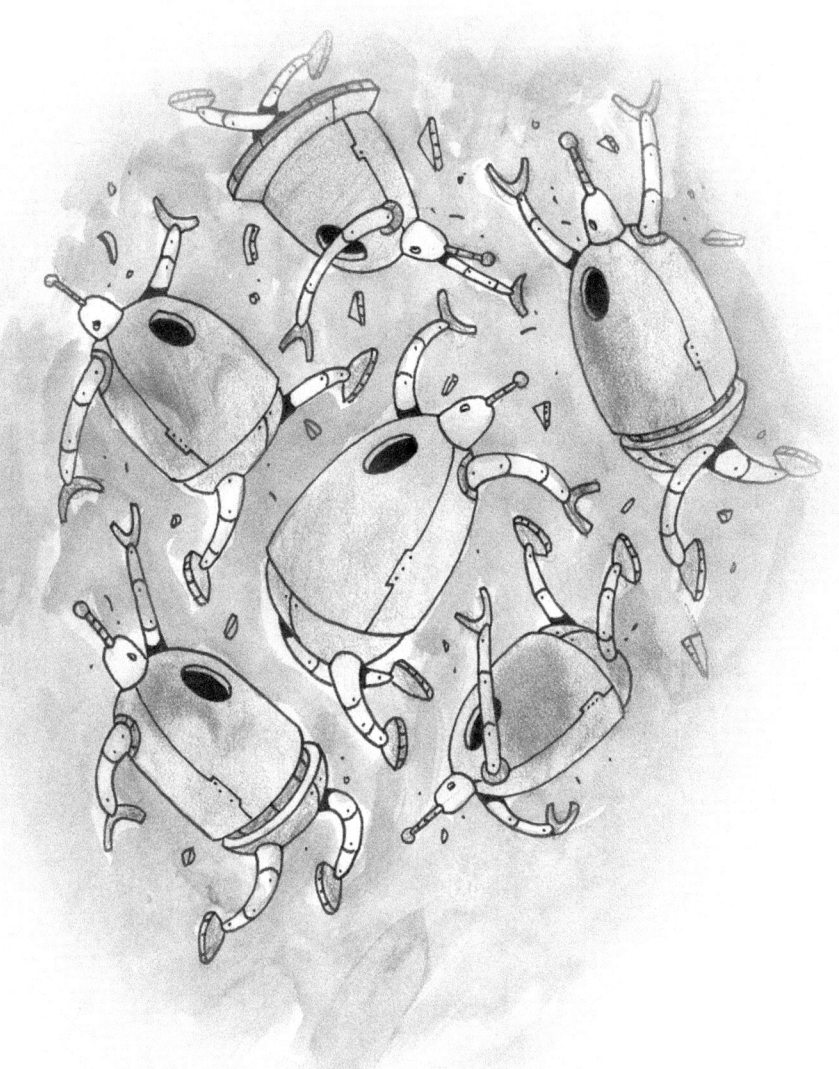

Many Jammers achieve jamming status to show other Jammers their jamming abilities and to assure their co-Jammers they have been authentically trained and reared in the knowledge of jamming (and not slamming) by a Jammer just like themselves, so as to set themselves in place upon the jamming social hierarchy.

Some Jammers jam to teach the jamming creed to the jamming youth.

Some Jammers jam to increase profit margins.

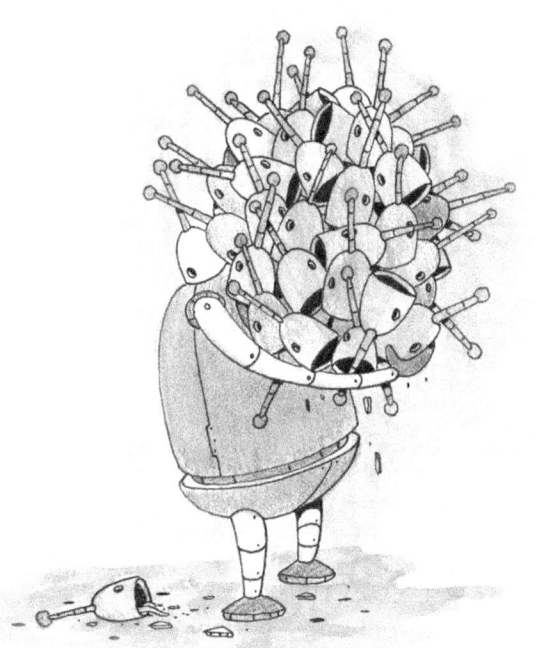

Many Jammers jam merely to spite the Slammers.

There are innumerable other reasons Jammers jam but most Jammers of all Jammers jam for the simplest reason of all to jam. They know no other way. They jam because they do not know how to slam, and visa versa. (This could be further elaborated upon, but an environment based on a mutual ignorance of this caliber should be self-explanatory.)

And here—inside the middle of this explanatory text—is the beginning of the Jammer Slammer story worthy of being told.

JAMMER
SLAMMER

AN EXPLANATORY TEXT

Thanks, Jenny.

ISBN 978-0-9838259-0-6

Second Printing

2019, 2012
R Nicholas Kuszyk
and Makeout Creek Books
Richmond, Virginia

www.rrobots.com
www.makeoutcreek.com

created by
R Nicholas Kuszyk

edited by
Andrew Blossom

 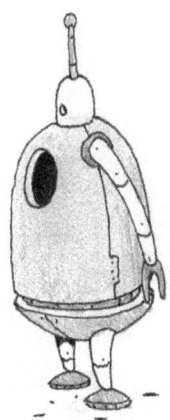

One day

all the Slammers disappeared.

During the duration of the exact moment the Slammers
disappeared, which lasted less than a second

Nothing Happened.

There was no movement.

There was no thought.

There was no emotional, physical, physiological or spiritual
reaction whatsoever.

Everything was perfectly still.

An unknowing peace, devoid of any action or reaction, filled the environment from brim to core with a serene emptiness and pure silence. For the first time in recorded Jammer history, Jammers did not jam.

But that moment passed.

Jammer senses quickly began to regain their hold but the magnificence of the disappearance of the Slammers was so significant a change that movement was not possible still in the first moment to follow. This experience was so foreign to the Jammers that they had no ability to nor knowledge of how to react physically. So the Jammers remained completely motionless in a state of perfectly balanced shock as they were internally confronted with an entirely new reality.

A reality without external comparison.

It was during this motionless nothing moment that the Jammers entered into a state of conscious spirituality they had never before considered or even subconsciously imagined. It was a moment of absolute equality. There were no fears, there were no resentments and there were no insecurities. And yet there were no absolutes. The hierarchies within the Jammer system dissolved and all jamming motivations evaporated. A calming self-realization warmly enveloped the Jammers and they felt for the first time what it was like to be truly themselves. There was nothing else. It was Jammer Bliss.

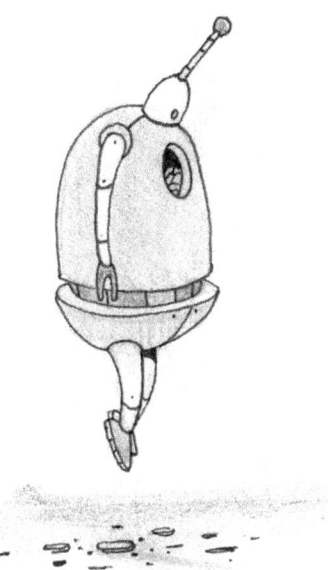

But that moment passed as well...

(It should be noted that the two aforementioned moments are of great significance to the balance and the trajectory of the new Slammerless environment created here. Without ample reflection upon these crucial moments of peace and equanimity, the intensity and severity of the events that next took place cannot be appreciated and absorbed to their fullest potential. These next moments were of destructive importance in that every subsequent action taken by a Jammer or by Jammer generations to come was influenced, inspired and/or informed by these moments, at least to a certain degree.)

...because all hell broke loose like a motherfucker.

(The Jammer Singularity Chaos Reaction)

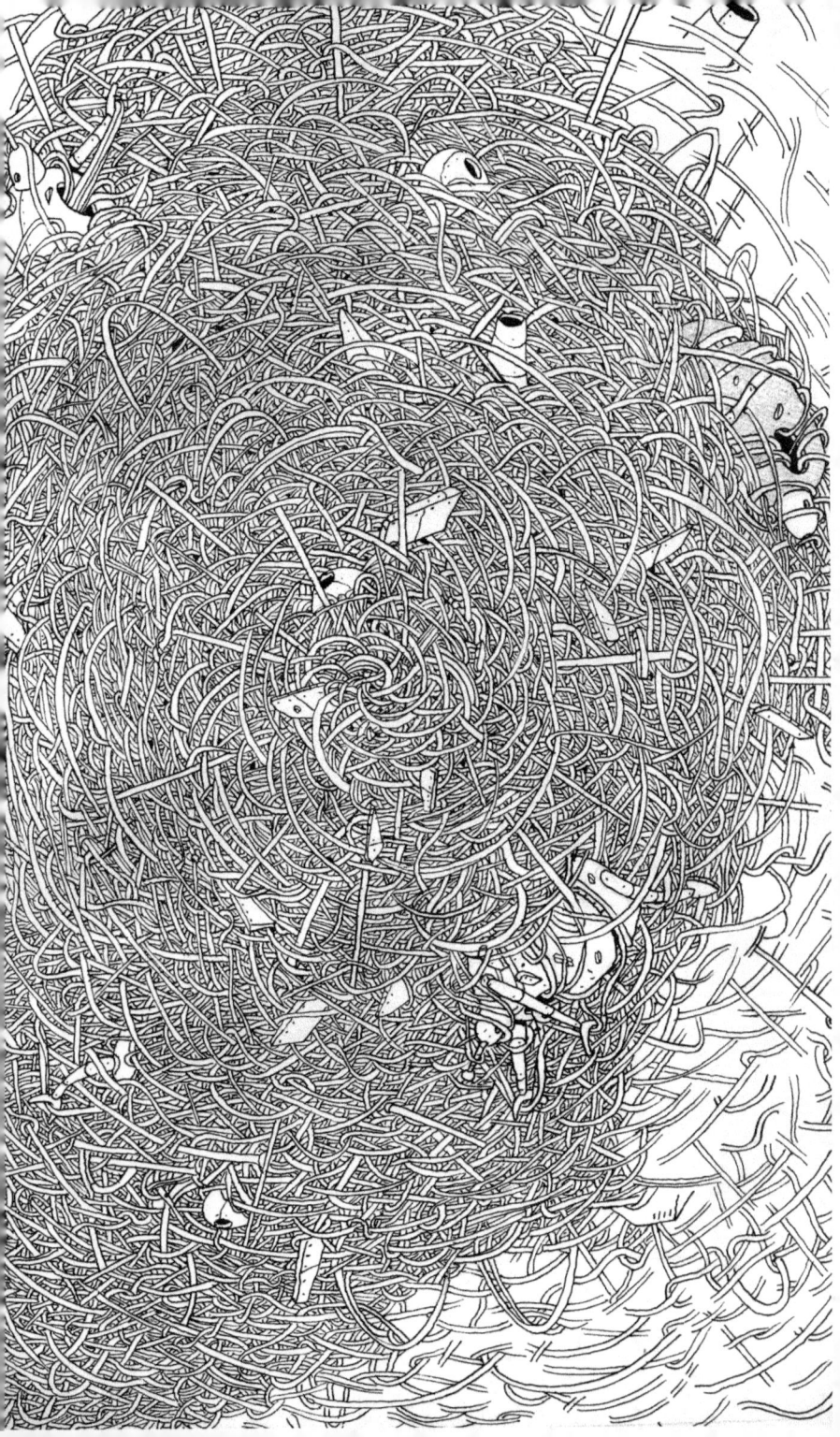

The notion of a Jammer singularity quickly became an overwhelming absolute and spiraled deep into the core of every Jammer spanning into eternity. Yet the parameters of this new void-like oneness were immediately filled with conflicting notions of self. Within seconds, the new singularity became far too much for most Jammers to process, while a chronological series of emotive projectionary backlashes spiraled exponentially out of control over the next unquantified period of time.

It is not clear what Jammer started the chain reaction, nor what that Jammer's initial action was, but it is known that the new Jammer Singularity Chaos Recoil started with a single Jammer beginning to jam involuntarily, as a reflex. Because this jamming occurred, a new Jammer foundation was set in place to incubate eventual social chaos.

Other Jammers began reacting to the new movement. And each Jammer's reaction created a reaction from another Jammer, and so on. Under normal circumstances these movements would have gone unnoticed, but within this new environment, without the shielding effect of the greater unified difference the Slammers had provided, and with Jammers having just experienced an eternal internal singularity spiral span, these reactions were magnified incredibly.

Before long, the small movements had become entirely new systems of jamming and multiple systems began to be developed.

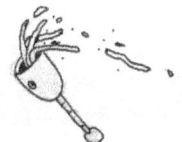

Singular
chus

Tiny physical flaws became a primary mode of separation.

New fragile systems quickly began to further embellish their differences and fracture so as to compete for a controlling share to secure their place in the new sociohistorical hierarchy.

The new groups eventually developed elaborately sophisticated jamming systems to separate themselves from others and attract new members in an increasingly competitive environment.

Some Jammers became highly ornate with little substance.

Some developed strict standards
of education, behavior and
jamming form.

Some Jammer groups had just a few core powerful members while others became enormous extended egalitarian Jammer families.

There were reports of as many as 4500 separate jamming sects at the height of this peacefully pluralistic period.

These groups evolved and devolved amongst one another, altering and integrating the new jamming idiosyncrasies for generations. The jamming traditions became less and less rooted in the old jamming as time passed. There came to be a variety of new modified jamming stereotypes that became more extreme during this period of tribalization and perpetual transformation. It is argued that the inherently self-balancing effect of this transitional stage created an environment that—however chaotic and disparate the transformations may have been—still managed to endure for centuries in relative social harmony.

Then, without warning, the jamming became violent.

The source and the catalyst of this violent jamming shift is unclear but certain histories point to a few small Jammer groups banding together in the vested interest of preventing one of the larger groups from dismantling them with its far grander jamming persuasiveness. Members of the larger and more persuasive group of modified Jammers, in an attempt to separate themselves from the alleged rogue Jammer alliance, and to acknowledge their evolved system as different from the old jamming way, changed their name and began calling themselves Mammers.

The Mammer Jammer violence killed off a large percentage of the population until just the two large groups remained. Most if not all of the surviving members of small jamming groups were persuaded by social order to denounce their allegiances and join one of the two dominant factions, the Mammers or the Jammers. It was now a Mammer Jammer environment. It is problematical to recount specifics of this period of violence due to their inherently graphic nature, while the exact details of Mammer Jammer evolution are difficult to interpret cohesively due to the destruction of most datable artifacts. What is most important to our knowledge of the Mammer Jammer environment is the event that abruptly interrupted this period.

The Slammers returned.